Brownilocks

and the
Three Bowls of Cornflakes

by Enid Richemont and Polona Lovšin

W
FRANKLIN WATTS
LONDON•SYDNEY

This story is based on the traditional fairy tale,
Goldilocks and the Three Bears, but with a
new twist. You can read the original story
in Hopscotch Fairy Tales. Can you
make up your own twisty tale?

First published in 2010 by
Franklin Watts
338 Euston Road
London
NW1 3BH

Franklin Watts Australia
Level 17/207 Kent Street
Sydney
NSW 2000

Text © Enid Richemont 2010
Illustrations © Polona Lovšin 2010

A CIP catalogue record for this book is available
from the British Library.

ISBN 978 1 4451 0177 4 (hbk)
ISBN 978 1 4451 0183 5 (pbk)

Series Editor: Melanie Palmer
Series Advisor: Catherine Glavina
Series Designer: Peter Scoulding

Printed in China

Franklin Watts is a division of
Hachette Children's Books,
an Hachette UK company
www.hachette.co.uk

Mum put out three

bowls of cornflakes.

3

"Let's go for a walk before breakfast," she said.

Brownilocks the bear was out
walking, too. She smelt the
cornflakes. "M-m-m, tasty,"
she thought, clambering in.

Brownilocks sat
on Dad's chair.
"Too hard!"
she growled.

So she tried
Mum's chair.
"Too soft!"
she moaned.

She went over to Sam's chair. "Just right!" she thought, reaching for Sam's cornflakes.

But ... **CRASH!**
Brownilocks was too
heavy and Sam's
chair snapped.

Brownilocks felt sleepy. She tried the biggest bed. "Too hard!" she grunted.

She tried the next bed. "Too bouncy!" she cried.

Then she tried the smallest bed.
"Just right!" she said, so she
climbed on and fell
fast asleep.

Mum, Dad and Sam came back
from their walk. Dad frowned.
"Who's been sitting in my chair?"
he asked.

"Who's been sitting in my chair?"
Mum gasped. But Sam yelled,
"Who's broken my chair and
eaten all my cornflakes?"

They looked all over the house.
"Who's been sleeping in our
bed?" cried Dad.
"And in this bed!" cried Mum.

"Hey! Look who's in my bed!"
yelled Sam. "And she's snoring!"

15

Brownilocks woke up,
ran downstairs and
outside. She ran across the
garden and into the woods.

"She was a nice bear,"
Sam sighed.
"I wish she'd come back."

Dad mended Sam's chair
and found a bean bag
for Brownilocks.

Next morning, Mum put out four
bowls of cornflakes – one for her,
one for Sam, one for Dad and
a big one for the bear.

Brownilocks soon came back
when she smelt the cornflakes.

"Here's your bowl," said Sam.

"Here's your bean bag," called Dad.

Brownilocks sat on Dad's chair.

"Try the bean bag," Dad said.

Brownilocks tried Sam's bowl.

"This one's bigger!"

said Sam.

Brownilocks scoffed up all the
cornflakes and slurped up
all the milk.

Brownilocks yawned. She thumped up the stairs and lay on Sam's bed.

Then Sam curled up with
Brownilocks and read her a story.

But Brownilocks longed to be
outside. She climbed out of
the window and ran
into the woods.

Sam wanted to see his new friend again. "Come back soon!" he cried.

Brownilocks liked the woods, but she also liked Sam – and the tasty cornflakes.

She did come back the very next day, and the day after that, and the day after that!

Puzzle 1

Put these pictures in the correct order.
Which event do you think is most important?
Now try writing the story in your own words!

Puzzle 2

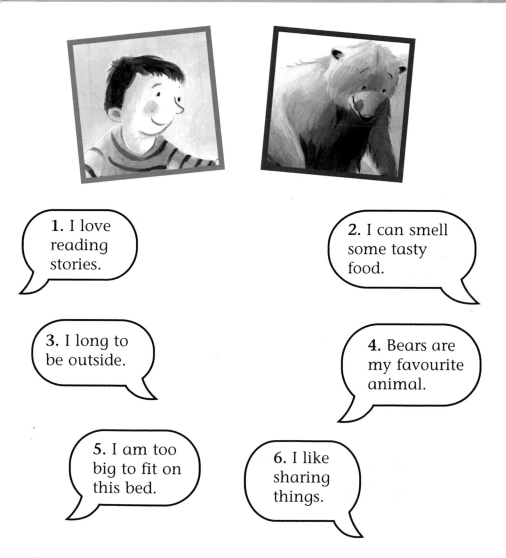

1. I love reading stories.

2. I can smell some tasty food.

3. I long to be outside.

4. Bears are my favourite animal.

5. I am too big to fit on this bed.

6. I like sharing things.

Choose the correct speech bubbles for each character. Can you think of any others? Turn over to find the answers.

Answers

Puzzle 1

The correct order is: 1e, 2f, 3c, 4d, 5a, 6b

Puzzle 2

Sam: 1, 4, 6

Brownilocks: 2, 3, 5

Look out for more Hopscotch Twisty Tales and Fairy Tales:

TWISTY TALES

The Three Little Pigs and the New Neighbour
ISBN 978 1 4451 0175 0*
ISBN 978 1 4451 0181 1

Jack and the Bean Pie
ISBN 978 1 4451 0176 7*
ISBN 978 1 4451 0182 8

Brownilocks and the Three Bowls of Cornflakes
ISBN 978 1 4451 0177 4*
ISBN 978 1 4451 0183 5

Cinderella's Big Foot
ISBN 978 1 4451 0178 1*
ISBN 978 1 4451 0184 2

Little Bad Riding Hood
ISBN 978 1 4451 0179 8*
ISBN 978 1 4451 0185 9

Sleeping Beauty – 100 Years Later
ISBN 978 1 4451 0180 4*
ISBN 978 1 4451 0186 6

FAIRY TALES

The Three Little Pigs
ISBN 978 0 7496 7905 7

Little Red Riding Hood
ISBN 978 0 7496 7901 9*
ISBN 978 0 7496 7907 1

Goldilocks and the Three Bears
ISBN 978 0 7496 7903 3

Hansel and Gretel
ISBN 978 0 7496 7904 0

Rapunzel
ISBN 978 0 7496 7900 2*
ISBN 978 0 7496 7906 4

Rumpelstiltskin
ISBN 978 0 7496 7902 6*
ISBN 978 0 7496 7908 8

The Elves and the Shoemaker
ISBN 978 0 7496 8543 0

The Ugly Duckling
ISBN 978 0 7496 8538 6*
ISBN 978 0 7496 8544 7

Sleeping Beauty
ISBN 978 0 7496 8545 4

The Frog Prince
ISBN 978 0 7496 8540 9*
ISBN 978 0 7496 8546 1

The Princess and the Pea
ISBN 978 0 7496 8541 6*
ISBN 978 0 7496 8547 8

Dick Whittington
ISBN 978 0 7496 8542 3*
ISBN 978 0 7496 8548 5

Cinderella
ISBN 978 0 7496 7417 5

Snow White and the Seven Dwarfs
ISBN 978 0 7496 7418 2

The Pied Piper of Hamelin
ISBN 978 0 7496 7419 9

Jack and the Beanstalk
ISBN 978 0 7496 7422 9

The Three Billy Goats Gruff
ISBN 978 0 7496 7420 5

The Emperor's New Clothes
ISBN 978 0 7496 7421 2